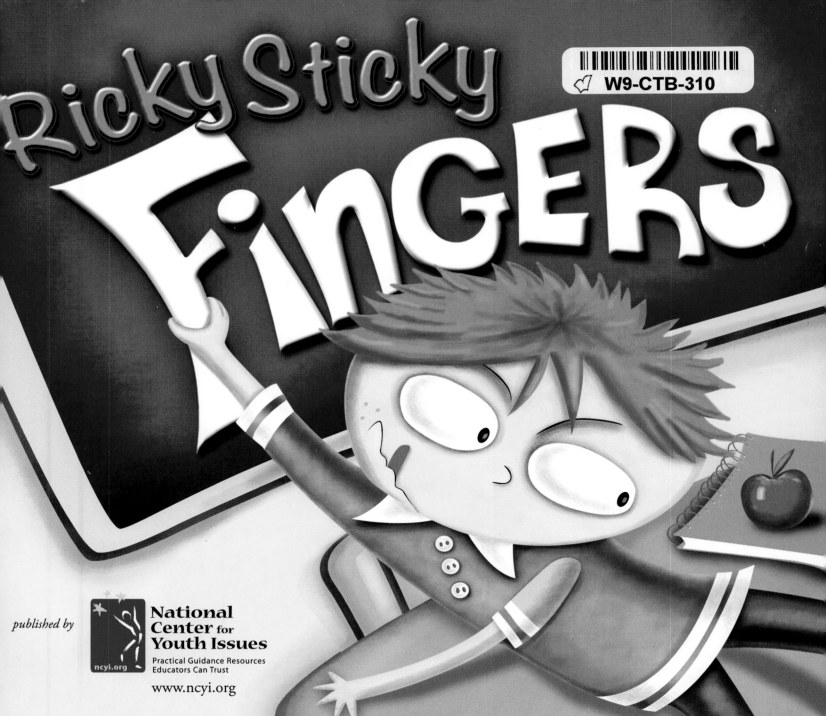

Ricky Sticky FiNGERS

W9-CTB-310

published by

National Center for Youth Issues

Practical Guidance Resources
Educators Can Trust

ncyi.org

www.ncyi.org

This book is dedicated to Katy, a phenomenal teacher!
–Julia

National Center for Youth Issues
Practical Guidance Resources
Educators Can Trust
ncyi.org

P.O. Box 22185
Chattanooga, TN 37422-2185
423.899.5714 • 866.318.6294
fax: 423.899.4547
www.ncyi.org

ISBN: 978-1-937870-08-9
© 2012 National Center for Youth Issues, Chattanooga, TN
All rights reserved.

Written by: Julia Cook
Illustrations by: Michelle Hazelwood Hyde
Design by: Phillip W. Rodgers
Contributing Editor: Beth Spencer Rabon
Published by National Center for Youth Issues
Softcover

Printed at RR Donnelley • Reynosa, Tamaulipas, Mexico • August 2016

My name is Ricky, but lately everyone's been calling me

"Ricky Sticky Fingers."

That's because sometimes, I take stuff that doesn't belong to me.

I steal!

When I see something that I really want,
I think, "Hey that could be mine!"
So I look both ways, reach out my hand,
and take it at just the right time.

4

If I ever get caught, I just pretend
that it wasn't me that took it.
A quick little lie is just what I need,
and lying helps me get through it!

Taking things that I want to have
at times can be very tricky.
But there's no way that I can help myself
Because all of my fingers are sticky!

A few days ago, I saw bubble gum in Marvin's desk at school. It wasn't just any bubble gum, it was my ABSOLUTE FAVORITE kind of bubble gum…

"Super Bubblerama!"

I thought about how good that gum would taste and how big the bubbles would be that I could blow.

Besides, ever since our principal sat in a wad of gum and ruined his pants, gum hasn't been allowed at school. So actually, I was doing Marvin a **BIG** favor by keeping him from being caught with it.

I looked both ways when no one was looking, and Marvin had gone to band. I took a deep breath and reached in his desk, and the gum just stuck to my hand!

I pulled my hand out of Marvin's desk and stuck the gum into my pocket.

When Marvin came back, he looked for his gum, so I convinced him he must have lost it.

On the way home from school that day, I stopped at the corner store to buy a bottle of triple-thick, double chocolate milk. On my way to the cooler in the back of the store, I walked by the toys, and there "it" was…the one thing that I wanted more than anything…a package of **"Slime Wads"** – the gooey balls that stick against walls when you throw them, and then they just…

OoZe doWn Onto the floor!

Slime Wads are cool.
They're not easy to find.

I just had to take them
so they could be mine!

I'd throw them at girls
to make them say,

"Icky!!"

It happened again!

My fingers got sticky!

is this Ricky's mom?

I stuffed the Slime Wads
into my pocket, paid for
my chocolate milk, and
headed out the door.

The next day at school, I forgot my gym shoes, so instead of playing basketball in PE, I had to sit on the bleachers and watch.

Sitting right next to me was Miss Rabon's special box…the one she keeps her clipboard, pens and whistle in. Sitting right on top of Miss Rabon's stuff was Dominic Russo's ninja guy. He'd gotten it for his birthday last week, and he accidentally brought it to school.

Miss Rabon told Dominic that the ninja guy was tired and needed to take a nap inside her special box while he was in P.E.

I looked at that ninja and thought, "How it could be?"
I needed that ninja, and he needed me!

When no one was looking, my fingers got sticky.
That ninja guy made me one happy Ricky!

At the end of P.E., Dominic went
to get the ninja guy out of the
box. When he found out it was
gone, he started to cry.

"Class, Dominic's ninja guy
woke up from his nap and
escaped from my special box!"
Miss Rabon said.

"Everyone start looking for him.
Make sure he isn't trying to hide out in one of your pockets."

When I got home from school, my mom gave me the "unibrow." You know, the look when both of her eyebrows go together. She only looks at me like that when she thinks I've done something wrong.

"Ricky," she said. "Today when I was doing the wash, I found this gum in your pocket. You know that we only let you chew sugarless gum! Where did you get this?"

"Oh," I said. "Marvin gave it to me."

"Are you sure?"

"YEP!"

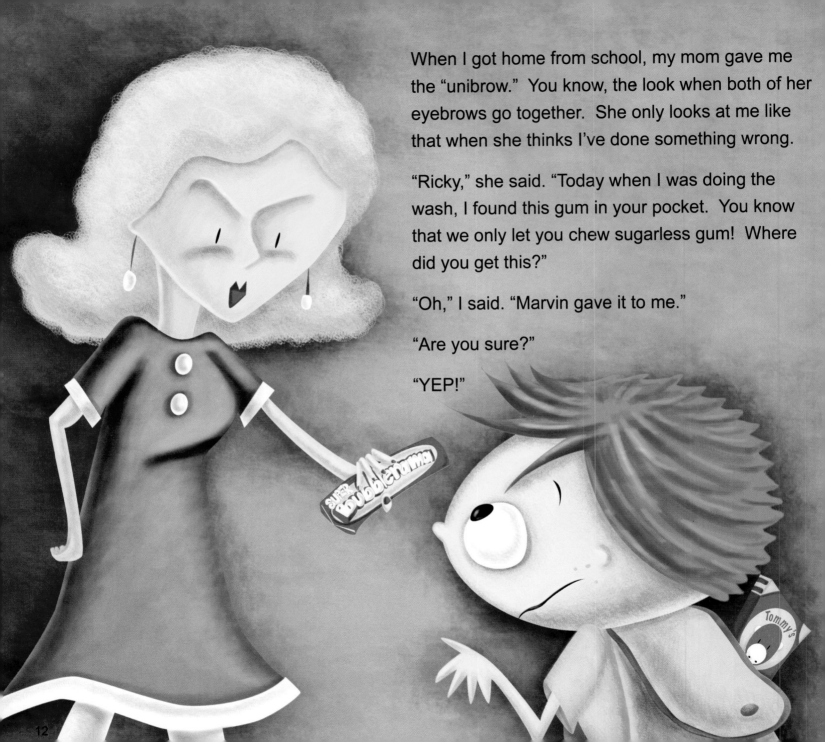

"Oh, and Ricky, I also found these Slime Wads in your room. Where did you get these?"

"Oh," I said. "I found them on the ground on the way home from school. Someone must have bought them at the corner store and then dropped them on the ground."

"Are you sure?"

"YEP!"

"Oh, and Ricky, Miss Rabon called from school today and asked us to be on the lookout for Dominic Russo's ninja guy. She said he escaped from her special box during P.E. Do you know anything about that?"

"No."

"Are you sure?"

"YEP!"

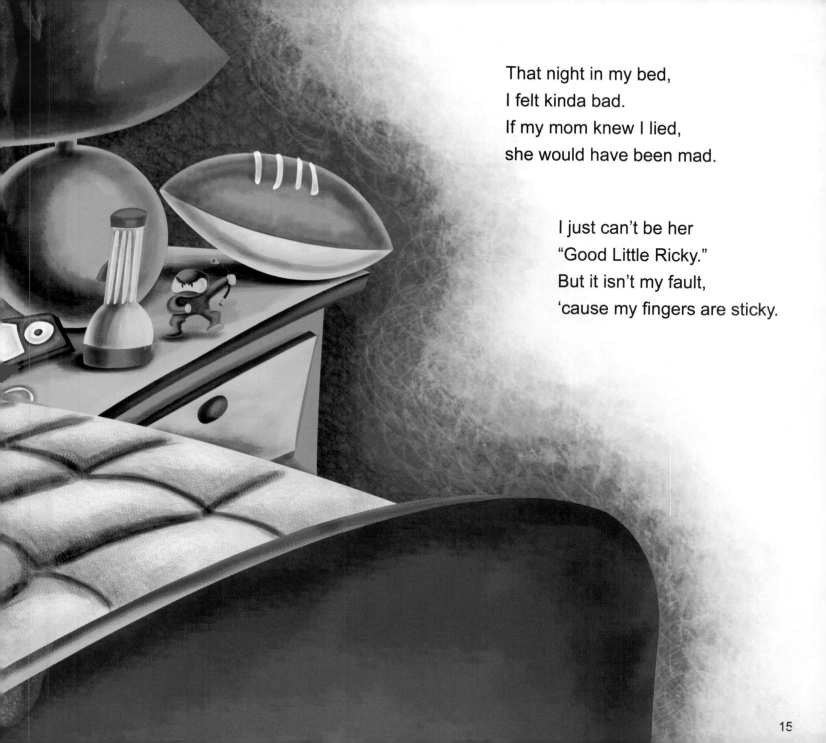

That night in my bed,
I felt kinda bad.
If my mom knew I lied,
she would have been mad.

I just can't be her
"Good Little Ricky."
But it isn't my fault,
'cause my fingers are sticky.

The next morning,
I went outside to the
garage to get my bike so I
could ride it to school.

My bike was **GONE!**

"Mom!!! My bike is gone!"
I screamed.

"Oh no, Little Ricky, it happened to you!

Your bike has been stolen. It's sad but it's true."

"But how could this happen? Who would do this to me?"

"Somebody thought that they needed your bike.

So they took it from you even though it's not right.

When kids
steal from stores,
the store owners

get MAD.

Then the prices go up,

and the
shoppers
feel

BAD.

When people steal things, they know that it's wrong.
But the bad inside wins, and the good plays along.

Inside they are thinking,
'That thing could be mine!'
And they're just not strong enough
to say 'NO' to the crime."

I felt so bad about my bike that I wanted to cry…

Then, I realized that I had made other people feel just like I do.

SO…I told my mom about Marvin's gum…

And about the Slime Wads…

And I even told her about Dominic Russo's ninja guy.

It was the hardest thing I have ever had to do!

I thought my mom would give me the unibrow again,
but she didn't…she **HUGGED ME!**

"You've made some mistakes,
but I still love you Ricky.

I know it seems hard when your
fingers are sticky.

Now is the time
to make these things right.

The good inside you needs
to put up a fight!"

So I went back inside my house and took all my money out of my piggy bank.

My mom drove me to school, but on the way, we stopped at the corner store. I walked in and told the store clerk that I had stolen the Slime Wads, and I paid her for them. She was **kinda** mad at me.

Then I bought Marvin a brand new pack of Super Bubblerama bubble gum. When I got to school, I gave it to him and told him what I did. He was **kinda** mad at me, too.

I found Dominic Russo and told him that his ninja guy decided to hang out in my pocket for a while, but then he got homesick and wanted to come back. Dominic was **REALLY MAD** at me at first, but then he got over it.

While I walked home from school I thought about my day.
The good inside me pushed the bad part away.

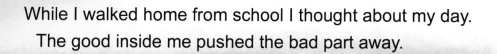

I felt great on the inside because I'd done the right thing.
Now I know that stealing is wrong, and it's mean.

There might still be days when my fingers get sticky.
I'll just have to tell myself, "Don't take that, Ricky!"

Now the good inside me tells the bad what to do.
And it feels great on the inside, to tell people the truth.

When I walked into my house, my mom said, "Hey Ricky, will you please take out the trash?"

"YEP."

A Note to Parents and Educators

When a person takes something that belongs to somebody else without permission, it is stealing. The stolen object could be as small as a piece of candy, or as big as a car. It could even be somebody else's words or ideas.

People steal for various reasons: A young child may not understand that taking something that they "want" is wrong. School-aged children understand the concept of right and wrong, but may not have the maturity or self-control needed to conquer temptation. Older children may choose to steal because of peer pressure in an attempt to "fit in." People may choose to steal because they are trying to fill the void of something that is missing in their lives, making them sad, angry, neglected or jealous. Some people steal because they feel they are "entitled." Others may not have enough respect for the rules and rights of others, they may steal simply for the thrill of getting away with it, or they may have developed some type of an addiction.

Regardless of the reason, stealing can have serious consequences because it hurts everyone involved. To counteract this problem, stealing <u>must</u> be addressed in a proactive manner. Here are a few tips:

- When a young child steals, parents need to do everything they can to help that child understand that stealing is wrong. (i.e. have the child return the stolen item, offer an apology for taking the item, use empathy to explain how stealing makes others feel, etc.)

- If you do not know who stole the item, but you have a strong suspicion, it may help to blame the item: i.e., "Class, Dominic's ninja guy woke up from his nap and escaped from my special box," Miss Rabon said. "Everyone start looking for him. Make sure he isn't trying to hide out in one of your pockets."

- With a school-aged child, it is important for that child to return the stolen item and offer to make amends. Explain to the child how and why stealing is wrong, and develop a consequence for a poor behavior choice.

- When teens steal, it's recommended that parents and educators follow through with stricter consequences. The embarrassment of having to return a stolen item and answering to authority can make for an everlasting lesson on why stealing is wrong.

- Further punishment, particularly physical punishment, is unnecessary and could make the child angry and more likely to engage in even more destructive and/or reactive behavior.

If a child has stolen on more than one occasion, there may be a deeper reason for this behavior, and professional help may been needed. If this happens, contact your family therapist or counselor, family physician, school counselor, religious counselor, or public support group.